MW01491535

COVER DESIGN BY TASALLY @ FIVERR.COM
COVER ART BY ARTISTRYWINGS @ FIVERR.COM
EMUS IN THE TRENCHES BY KLUKVAUSUAL @ FIVERR.COM
EMUS AT SUNSET BY IESHAHMALIK @ FIVERR.COM
NEWSPAPERS DESIGNED BY GAYANCHAMIRA @ FIVERR.COM
PHOTO'S SOURCED FROM PIXABAY.COM

CONTACT THE AUTHORS:
JABRYDEN.GODADDYSITES.COM

PUBLISHED BY J.A. BRYDEN

"If we had a military division with the bullet-carrying capacity of these birds it would face any army in the world...They can face machine guns with the invulnerability of tanks. They are like Zulus whom even dum-dum bullets could not stop."

MAJOR G.P.W MEREDITH

Yes. Australia really did declare war on Emus.

Yes. The emus won.

And it's about time we gave them a voice.

This is their story..

LETTERS FROM THE EMU WAR

CORRESPONDENCE FROM THOSE WHO
CLAIMED VICTORY IN THE GREAT EMU WAR
OF 1932

J.A. BRYDEN

CHRIS PARK

INTRODUCTION

This book was written for those brave soldiers who fought in the most embarrassing war in Australian history. Almost one hundred years ago (1932) in Campion Western Australia they fought for their right to live. Although they rose victorious they lacked the opposable thumbs needed to record their historic achievement. And so their story lies forgotten by the very people they defeated.

Today they watch closely from the roadside as travellers of the dusty highways nervously pass them by unsure if they will leap without warning into the oncoming traffic. Some are found in wildlife parks tilting their heads in curious fashion, again making people nervous. Others have travelled to other countries, possibly with the intent of becoming "diplomats" or "foreign correspondents." Regardless of their reasons the look in their double eyelid eyes, I believe, is one of superiority. They say dolphins are the most intelligent animal on the planet but I sometimes question that notion. For out of the millions and millions of species that have walked (and swam) the earth, only one has been to war with mankind...and won.

Today their army is the 5th largest in the world and given enough time their numbers will increase even more. They have such a strong presence in Australia and their story deserves to be heard.

I for one welcome our soon to be Dromaius Novaehollandiae overlords.

PREFACE

September 16, 1932
From the desk of high command
Dictated by Cleary Feathers
To Edward R Long-toe. For his eyes alone.

Edward. While the Court of Mobs have found you not guilty, I on the other wing hold you in the highest contempt. While they cannot prove that you took those pebbles there could be no one else. Pebbles like that do not just end up in the wings of the poor. Which brings me to my next point. The High Command, meaning myself, have noticed that one in five of our kind have gizzards full of pebbles but no fruit. As you know, one cannot exist without the other. Therefore, I am reactivating you and in the name of the All Feather giving you higher command of a mob. You will take this mob west. The cousin who enjoys a good joke every morning informs us that we must travel west to the land of fruit and caterpillars. This notion is intriguing to say the least and odds are this is a head in the sand mission but on the off chance the land of fruit and caterpillars exists, we cannot risk standing idly by.

I know you have your duties and an incoming family but those will have to be the responsibility of your wife...

1

THE EXPEDITION

"You can have all the pebbles in the world but it won't put fruit on the table"

Edward R Long-toe

FOOD FOUND WEST

The land of fruit & caterpillars is close to being confirmed as the high mob has placed **Captain Edward Long-toe** in charge of the westward expedition expecting to leave in a few days. Long-toe was part of a recent scandal involving some missing pebbles but was cleared of all charges. Although some members of the mob believe him to be guilty they have little choice but to accept the outcome and hope we will all be whistling his praises if this expedition is proved successful. Another key member of the expedition is **William J Whistlebeak**. A researcher, historian and scientist who has made the controversial announcement of keeping a record of not only the expedition itself but all of our history as well. "How can we be respected as a species if we keep everything to ourselves." He said in an interview with Tree Hugger Weekly. "If our history is only passed from beak to ear how will future generations know its reliability?" Once the expedition was announced it did not take long to fill all the positions as volunteers were lining up from everywhere. As of now the mob stands at twenty fifteen strong. We asked the High Mob why they requested such a high number but they declined to respond. While our nation waits for the expedition to leave we are aware of its historic significance. We can feel our burdens lifting, so much so that some believe we will be able to join our cousins in the sky.

Column by Deidre Gizzardwing

★ ★★★ ★★★ ★ ★★★

TREE HUGGER DEFEATS

Legendary Tree Hugger Kev took down Bouncer Aces in a match so intense it left spectators watching in eerie silence. The fight lasted twice as long as the screechers predicted. Despite the clear difference in weight class Kev was very inventive with his style. At one point he picked up two prickly ant eaters by their noses and wielded them like weapons. Aces got in a plentiful amount of kicks before eventually succumbing to the mighty roar and claw of the victor, Tree Hugger Kev. In a post fight interview Aces referred to his opponent as "a cuddly demon that will not be

BOUNCER TO TAKE TITLE

underestimated again." Kev is already preparing for the next championship and is planning to move even further up the weight classes. "I want to make all my opponents afraid of me." said a confident Kev "Standing in my presence will be unbearable." Throughout the tournament Kev has been relentless and shows no sign of easing up, even in his personal life. His passion for the fight is what helped him gather so many followers. We congratulate him on the win and will be sure to follow his career closely.

Column by Arnold Sly

September 21st, 1932
   From William J Whistlebeak
   to Henry Hookwing

Dear Henry

While my companions write to their wives and families speaking of our expedition, I find myself more interested in writing to you. I do not plan to neglect my family entirely and will write to them as time permits but for now my work takes precedence...our work takes precedence. I ask that you take the information provided in this letter and compile it for safe keeping upon my return. Every letter that follows, do the same. My research must be preserved and you are the one I trust most with the task.

As you are aware, Captain Edward R Long-toe leads the expedition. A tall attractive male with a glistening beak that many would say is wing-crafted by the All Feather himself. He is highly respected by the mob of twenty and twenty, myself included. No one is more optimistic than he in what we hope to achieve. Finding food for our nation is the priority but as you know, I am one of science and discovery. It is my hope that I will discover new species and learn of their culture as well as new fauna and landscapes. There are many possibilities and I look forward to sharing my discoveries with you and everyone back home.

We are but a few moments into our journey and I have already mastered the ability to write and walk simultaneously. This will make things much more easy for me. Any thought that comes to mind I will jot down swiftly and efficiently. Thoughts, they are wonderful are they not? Ideas transpire from them as well as solutions to problems. Observations are compiled with them. Many a thought moves through my mind even now as we travel across the unchanging landscape. Every hill we climb we are greeted with an identical view as the previous one. The only thing that gives us confidence that we are not caught in some sort of loop are the looks we are given from the featherless ones in the trees as we pass. Have they not seen a mob so large before? Evidently not. I conversed briefly with one and it would appear food is scarce out here as well. They tell us we are dreaming and appear somewhat confident that there is nothing but sand and breeze where we are headed. However, I question the certainty of those who haven't left their trees since All Feather knows when but I digress, I have let my thoughts wander again. The sun will rise and fall then rise once more by the time we arrive where we are headed. I would have much preferred the High Mob name it something more fitting other than the land of fruit and caterpillars. Naming a scientific expedition after hopes and hearsay does not sit well with me. I wish to record it under a different name for the Mob records but that may leave some confused. Make no mistake, what we are doing is historic and it is an honour to be apart of it.

There is little more I can say at this time for our journey has only just begun. I will be sure to meet as many of the Mob as possible and learn their stories, for understanding what drives one to join an expedition such as this is the beginning of understanding what makes our nation so great. As a whole we are willing to step up and seek solutions to any problem, small or big. Why is that? Why do we care? Surely there is more to it than just putting food in our bellies? These are the questions I hope to answer.

Send my regards to those at home and if time permits check on my dear Maggie.

William J Whistlebeak

Dearest Celene

As I dip my toe into the ink to write to you I am reminded of my father. He would spend a day writing correspondence to his uncle who he had not seen for some time. Day after day he would write. I once asked him how did he know the letters would reach his uncle, he smiled and told me, if I spent less time with my head in the sand and more time looking to the All Feather I would trust. I find myself now much like my father trusting that this letter finds you in good health.

It has been many days since I was given command of this odd ball group. At first I thought my mission to be nothing more than a head in the sand dream, something akin to thinning our population or sending us on a wild cousin chase.

It vexes me that High Command would give me such a post knowing that we have children to keep warm. These early months are critical. There is a part of me that knows they are my children and my everything but a part of me will be sad that I will not be present to imprint on them...How will they know that I am their father?

It brings me some joy that William has joined us on this expedition. He is one of our finest minds. He has the capacity to count to high numbers. I once saw him count over twenty hoppers. It was one of the greatest things that I have seen in my life.

The other day I watched in amazement as he organised the entire Mob to move in a single direction. His mind is the sun. It is always exact.

I know that in some small way this command was the High Mob's way of punishing me. Through out the entire ordeal with the pebbles, while it was clear that I was found innocent of no wrong doing, our family has been punished beyond what one would consider reasonable.

My hope is that while I am gone with the Mob, you and our children will be left in relative peace.

Please ensure that you rotate our children regularly. I know you have seen me do it often enough but it's not as easy as it sounds. Rotate too often and you will lose the good spot. Don't rotate enough and one of our children will surely die.

As I look at the Mob I can see that the All Feather did not bless me with the best and brightest. Far too many with their heads in the sand, the others are pebble seekers, head bobbers and side runners. Although I am certain they look at me with contempt I am satisfied with the knowledge that I could kick them to death.

I hope that in time I can earn their respect and do something with this mob. I can feel there is something here.

Each day I look upon the item you gave me and each time it brings me closer to you with all my heart and feathers.

Edward R Long-toe

September 23rd, 1932
From John Feathers to his wife

My dearest Greta

I pray this letter finds you in good health and eases your mind knowing that I too am the same at present. I trust the children are in good spirits and are keeping their heads above the sand. I know my decision to leave on this expedition has been a strain on us both but I pray that one day you will understand why I had to be apart of it. The journey out west has been long and treacherous but my thoughts are of you and the children with every step I take away from home.

We arrived here early evening and have yet to see the plentiful food that Edward has spoken of but its smell travels on the breeze much like our cousins in the sky.

Mere moments ago Edward restrained a few of us trying to run ahead. I can understand their lapse in judgment. Our stomachs grumble and although we are indeed hungry we must think of the bigger picture.

As I write this letter I hear the many complaints of Percival. He does not wish to be here but given the time I am convinced Edward will turn him into a fine soldier.

William on the other hand spends most of his time writing. He keeps notes on every little thing, no matter how insignificant it may seem. He has also been known to steal the quills right off our backs. Many find it amusing until they are on the receiving end themselves. He is very serious about his work and is a strange but entertaining addition to the expedition.

Tomorrow will be a historic day for us. We will finally head into the land of fruit and caterpillars promised to us by the mighty All Feather. Soon we will have enough provisions to supply our nation a dozen times over. We will unify once more and no one will go hungry again. The path we take will not be easy but I trust Edward. He is an impeccable leader with great skill and prowess. I have seen first wing his ability to reason with both Bouncers and Hoppers alike. He will be ready for any negotiations with the locals if and when it comes to that.

As there are no shortages of quills here I will write to you again when I have more news.

Greta, my love, I miss you and the children dearly and I count the days until I will return to you safely.

John Feathers

October 27th, 1932
From John Feathers to his wife

My dearest *Greta*

Time has not permitted me to write to you until now and I do not wish you to think I have forgotten you. You and the children are always in my thoughts. I know you have taken on much of my fatherly duties and I pray the All Feather would lend you the strength to continue until my return.

We have all been busy out here in the west. So much has been happening I would not have enough paper to mention it all to you now. There is more than enough food here to feed us for a lifetime. Still William seems disappointed that there has been minimal fruit and only the odd caterpillar. It may not be what we were promised but the All Feather has indeed provided us with all we need. The food is like nothing I have ever tasted before. It crumbles in my beak and leaves me thirsty but also wanting more. The supply is bountiful but there is something unnatural about it. It appears to be organised. We think by the locals. Some question if it is right to take but their concerns are silenced by the call of their stomachs. Edward is under a lot of pressure from those who wish to do their own thing but he is a great leader and is doing well under the circumstances. Our captain is more respected everyday.

It is my hope that I may bring you and the children here someday. Words cannot do justice for the beauty of this place. Food as far as the eye can see and a unique smell in the air that travels on the breeze from the west. I conversed with a bouncer who spoke of an endless lake you cannot drink from. We may see it when the rain ceases and if Edward allows. We have limited recreation time as we have begun harvesting the outer area of food. The work is hard but rewarding as we are encouraged to taste what we collect. At our current rate we should be scheduled to return within the month. Hold on a little longer, Dear Greta. Our sacrifice will reap great reward. May the All Feather bless and keep you.

John Feathers

October 27th, 1932
From William J Whistlebeak to
Henry Hookwing

Dear Henry

I must apologise. I have spent so long filling my journal with notes on this wonderful place that I have neglected in writing to you. As I have mentioned previously, I ask that you preserve the letters I send so my research may not be all for naught in the off chance that something happens to me.

This new land has so much to offer. It was as dry as home for quite a while but that did not last. It has been raining so long now I almost forget what the dusty earth felt like under my toes. We currently take turns keeping dry beneath the trees but that is of little importance.

It is not the bountiful supply of food I find so remarkable, it is the way it is organised. Almost like we were expected. Food lined up in rows for us to take at will. I am yet to complete my count but at first glance there is easily enough for each of us to take a row and fill our bellies twenty times over. We have all taken a small sample of this new food. It is unlike any food we have ever tried before. I believe the locals call it wheat. It is far from the fruit and caterpillars we were promised but it will feed our nation and that is the purpose of Captain Long-toe's expedition.

As for the locals, we have seen them watching us with curious eyes. They vary in height and appear to have very small necks. Some shake their arms with passion. It is clearly some kind of greeting. Long-toe is recommending we keep our distance for the time being or at least until we are certain they pose no threat to us. I however am intrigued by them and already devising ways to communicate. I approached them travelling down one of their wide paths but they merely blasted a loud sound resembling our cousins of the lakes. They sleep in shelters made of trees and some other material I am yet to identify. Sometimes smoke will rise from them and yet somehow they do not burn. I wish to understand why that is.

I may approach such a shelter given the chance though I do question how wise of an action that would be. Long-toe might not be pleased but I believe I can convince him to reconsider his position. He and I see differently as we are on our own expeditions in a way. Mine being one of discovery and his being one of providing for our hungry nation. He is cautious of creating tension between the locals and ourselves while I believe there is only true discovery when risk is involved. Like travelling to the west without bringing any pebbles. How could we possibly know there would be plenty in a foreign land? We did not but there is more here than anywhere I have been before. How I wish you could see this wonderful land for yourself, Henry. It truly is a marvel to the eyes.

I will make sure you receive a sample of wheat and ask you to drop some to my dear Maggie. Watch her closely, Henry. Many a male will try and steal her from me while I am away but you I trust.

William J Whistlebeak

Dearest Mother

It would be remiss of me not to mention the change of heart I feel at this time. I am blessed to be apart of such a journey. I have never seen so much food. This truly is the land of fruit and caterpillars. I overheard some of the Mob talking about something called wheat and barley. They must be the scientific names for this new food we have discovered. You will soon have some to taste for yourself as preparations have begun for sending some home to our families to try.

You will be pleased to know that I have made a few friends on this expedition. Reginald, Norman and Cecil. They are a funny bunch of larrikins. I am certain Father would disapprove of them but they make for great company. Cecil has been perfecting his jokes on our laughing cousins. It is quite amusing to watch him fail more than he succeeds. I do not know what response one would expect from things such as 'why did the Mob cross the dessert? To get to the land of fruit and caterpillars.' We laugh sympathetically but he has a long way to go if he wants to succeed in a career of comedy. I think of you often out here. While the adventure brings many a smile I do miss you and home. I have heard that some of us may be sent home within the month however that may just be a rumour spreading through the Mob. There is also talks of migrating here as the food source is plentiful and with all the rain that has been falling more may grow. In the end we have found what we need but the Captain is still deciding on the best way to distribute it. Either way, our troubles may soon be over.

Percival Headsand

Dearest Celene

Each day I look upon the item you gave me, it brings me great comfort to know that it belonged to such an outstanding mob member as your father. I write to you with a shaking foot and my feathers high in the air. I cannot help but to dance in a circle and move my wings about.

After many moons of travel we found it...the land promised by our great All Feather, the land of fruit and caterpillars.

I had long thought the High Mob had sent us out here to diminish the mobs due to the lack of food. As my father used to say 'you can have all the pebbles in the world but it won't put fruit on the table.'

William is certain this was some kind of end world, that we had died due to lack of food or due to lack of interest. I have never been more happy to hear William's words when he said ' I think we have it.' While I pray to the All Feather as a member of the Mob I should admit I have not heard the stories of the land of fruit and caterpillars since I first left the egg but recalling it now, this must be the land.

As we venture further in I have never seen such a bounty. Though I am not partial to this new food , I certainly will eat it to pass the time. Never in my wildest dream would I see such a strange but wondrous sight. William said there are at least twenty and twenty and twenty and twenty rows of wheat, as they call it.

What brings William's head out of the sand more so than anything is the knowledge that the All Feather does in fact hate the Hoppers. There are strong leafless trees that appear to have grown around the grain to prevent the

Hoppers from getting through but easy enough for a mob member to push through.

The first few days I will admit that I gave the mob liberty to eat and enjoy. This in fact was not the smartest thing I have ever done as not long after twenty of the twenty and twenty rows were gone. It is fitting that that they should eat, they have in fact journeyed this far on a wing and a prayer. We found the strangest thing the other day, water, while we are used to seeing water in the great lakes. This was interesting, water in tiny puddles. Normally drinking from a puddle is not the most pleasant of experiences but these tiny puddles, Cerene, in my all of my life, I have never tasted water so wonderful. Tomorrow William wants to make contact with the locals. They seem peaceful and odd creatures living in thick bushes and staring at us all day. They seem to come out after we have fed waving their hands in the air. Perhaps this is some kind of greeting and gesture. Tomorrow William will try the same. We hope to make communication with them as while there are not many of them, I see no reason they cannot enjoy this wonderful land with us. Within time I will send for you. With each day you are near to me as I stare at the item, with all my heart and feathers.

Captain Edward R Long-toe

The land of fruit and caterpillars

A lone Short-neck and his hut

2

EMUS AT WAR

"We shall not surrender. We are the Mob. We do not stick our heads in the sand. We run in all directions as all directions lead to war."

Edward R Long-toe

SHORT-NECKS DECLARE WAR

MORE MISSING STRIPPERS

The case of the missing Stripers is a mystery that begun shortly after the peace treaty that was signed by our two great nations. Three more went missing this week and we still have no clue where they have gone and who is responsible. Lawrence Wynd has been working the case since the beginning. A Howler who has solved every mystery put before him. "I've got a nose for these things." Said Wynd "It may take a little longer than usual but I will get to the bottom of it." Whilst some are losing faith in Wynd others look to his perfect record and pray to the All Feather that this mystery will soon be solved.

Column by Norman McWhistle

The expedition was ambushed yesterday while grazing on the western plains. "They made no effort to negotiate" said Long-toe "So we have little choice but to fight." Long-toe has reassured the mobs that he will do everything in his power to end this war as quickly as possible. "There is little known about the Short-necks military but given the time they will reveal their weaknesses." Four of the mob were killed in the attack and even more are expected to succumb to their wounds. What we do know of the enemy is that their preferred method of attack is to spit countless golden pebbles out of something that imitates the sound of our laughing cousins. Some of the mob have suffered temporary hearing loss due to the very loud sound. The High Mob is yet to publicly reveal what the Mob's next actions will be

but we have heard from alternate sources that reinforcements will be deployed to the west and there are talks of conscription if necessary. If that is the case then the bouncers will be called in to defend our homes. Something that has not happened since the Great Featherless Crusade.

Column by Deidre Gizzardwing

★★★★

Joke of the day

What do you call a lazy baby Bouncer?

A pouch potato.

★★★★

SILENT LAUGHNING COUSIN

Ethel Bluewing is known for her beautiful laugh but that is something she has not done in a very long time. "I need a break." She said "I know I was hatched for this but sometimes the sun and the rain are just not that funny." Despite encouragement coming from everyone in the community, Ethel's reluctance stays strong. (More on page 3)

PERSONAL COLUMN

If you like fresh caterpillars and chasing clouds full of rain. If you're cautious of howlers. If you have half a brain. If you dream of one day flying to a land far away then I am the one that you've looked for. Let's

November 3rd, 1932
   Lieutenant Edward R Long-toe's
   public address

To the High Command and the mobs, to the young, the old and all those who worship the All Feather. On this day the world has changed. On this day we will remember that our lives will never be the same.

The great nations of the Mob and the Short-necks of the great western plain were at peace, and as the solicitation of the western plain the mob was brought into the valley, the heart of the land of fruit and caterpillars. This was to be the first of peace summits and the start of the long journey of our two nations. But the Short- necks appeared and began to spit pebbles at us. They spat pebbles to the left. They spat pebbles to the right. They spat pebbles at such speeds many of the mob stood in fear. On this day four of the mob were killed. Thomas Wing-toe, able footman. Karl Stiffbeak, able footman. Reginald S Head-twitch, second Wingrunner and Earnest R Eggsland, able footman.

The Short-necks have asked us to leave! the Short-necks have asked us to surrender! I have been asked as the highest ranking mob leader to give our reply. I say to you as I said to them. Come what may, the Mob Nations never flinch! Surrender? Never! We shall not surrender! We are the Mob! We do not stick our heads in the sand! We run in all directions as all directions lead to war! We will fight them in the valley! We will fight them in the streams, in the forests and in the sand! We will never surrender a single grain of sand! A single inch of land!

We are one mob now! But is the nation of the mobs made from one mob? I call on every Mob who believe as I do. That we have the right to live and anyone to deny us that right, may the All Feather have mercy on you as we will show you none!

Lieutenant Edward R Long-toe

November 3rd, 1932
From William J Whistlebeak
to Henry Hookwing

Dear Henry

Forgive me as I skip over the pleasantries as a lot has happened out west. The expedition started well but as of yesterday we are under threat of war if not already in it. It appears the locals are threatened by our presence here. They set up an ambush for us. I was close to the front when it began. Without warning we were hit with so many pebbles it was impossible to count them all. The sound was so loud it put the fear of the All Feather into many of us. It was a sound I will never forget. It resembled our laughing cousins but with a much deeper tone. When the sound ceased a series of strange clicks would follow before starting again. The experience was horrifying for most but I as a bird of science and discovery had to compose myself. I had to be as brave as an angered blue cousin and take note of all that happened. Someone has to keep a record of it. Lieutenant Long-toe has proven yet again he is the right bird for the job. His quick decision for us all to scatter saved many lives but sadly we lost four today. Karl Stiffbeak, Tomas Wing-toe, Earnest R Eggsland and Reginald S Head-twitch. I will be sure to send a melon to their widows.

The Lieutenant has instructed the Mob to only visit water supplies in pairs. We currently stay between high hills to remain hidden from those that wish to do us harm. The Mob has been broken into smaller ones, each with their own lookouts. Naturally the taller ones are appointed to this command as they have the best visibility. I would like to take this moment to remind you of the importance of my work. In the past our kind have leaned away from written records. We memorise our history and pass it on from beak to ear. I am the first to attempt the change and I deem it worth the risk. I anticipate your wonder of this risk I speak of. The answer is simple. Plagiarisers, thieves, those who wish to rewrite history. As long as we keep our records safe the truth will always come to light.

I send with this letter a hollow pebble for you to examine. As you can see it is indeed hollow and smells of a strange smoke. I will continue to send you things to place aside for when we open our collectory. A place where many can come to learn of the wonders from the west.
I appreciate all you are doing for my work and my family, Dear Henry. I hope this war will not be so far spread as to reach our home.

William J Whistlebeak

4th November, 1932
From John Feathers to his wife

My Dearest Greta

It is with a heavy heart I write to you this day. I have no words to soften the news I am about to share. While grazing in the plains a few strides from where we recently harvested supplies we were attacked unprovoked and without warning. If not for Edward's quick action we would have suffered many casualties. He assessed the threat and commanded us to scatter. I could not see our attackers but they left behind many odd shaped pebbles. William has studied them extensively but not even I could understand the scientific terms he was muttering. We were all but certain of peace with the locals but it is clear that is no longer the case. War has been declared and I am afraid I may not return for some time.

An expedition to feed our nation was never going to be an easy one but I welcome the challenge. Much like our inability to fly it is but an obstacle to greatness. Many have underestimated us before and we always won the day. This will be no different.

Edward has sent word to High Command awaiting instruction. He has spent a lot of time by himself since then. I believe he is going through every possible scenario. That is what I would do. Honestly, those twenty minutes I spend before sleeping each night I do much the same.

We often see Edward holding the shiniest of pebbles. It is too big to put in ones mouth so I believe it has some sentimental value. I have an inkling of it's origin but I feel it is something he does not wish to share with the troops. Whatever it may be we trust him. The silent leader that never fails us.

Times are changing. For better, for worse, the outcome we are yet to know. Just remember what I have said. We always win the day. Always.

I do not wish you to worry, my dear wife. We are protected under the wings of the All Feather. Before long I will return home to you and the children and will once again resume my fatherly duties.

I think of you always.

John Feathers

The item mentioned in Edward's letters. It is believed that Edward's father in-law was once involved in an unfortunate incident involving a Short-neck travelling through the Australian outback. Barely making it out with his life he carried the item with him as a reminder of his luck. He passed it onto his daughter, Celene, who then passed it onto Edward before he left in search of the land of fruit and caterpillars.

One of the many advantages the Mob had over their enemy was the ability to dig trenches at a much faster rate. Edward R Long-toe would often encourage the Mob to think outside the norm and it is rumoured that they once donned the Short-neck uniform in an attempt to infiltrate the enemy. We were unable to find any evidence of this within the gathered correspondence but this could be due to concerns of possible vulnerabilities within the postal service. Here in lies the problem. All theories are pure speculation.

November 5th, 1932
From Percival Headsand to his Mother

Dearest Mother

I write this letter in earnest to plead with you for help. Please would you ask Father to use his connections to have me sent back home. This is not due to my distaste of the food or the primitive sleeping conditions. We are at war and your little chick does not belong here. We were attacked by a pair of giant laughing cousins that spat shinny pebbles at us. The Mob lost many of its members and the enemy plucked the feathers from our backs to place on their heads. We are utterly humiliated and I want no part of this.

I know Father and I are not on the best of terms but I would do anything to repair our relationship if it means that I could return home.

I keep this letter short as I hope to tell you more of my time away on my return. May the All Feather keep you safe.

Your only son,

Percival Headsand

November 6th, 1932
From Edward R Long-toe to his wife

Dearest Celene

I am pleased to hear that my words have made it around the mobs and I understand there are those who think I should return home to help in the effort of inspiring and raising pebbles for the war, but I cannot. I am harkened back to the words my father told me when I was newly hatched. He told me that the Mob moves fast and each day I would try to run as he would, as all soldiers do. However my legs had not yet developed the skills. The others would mock me but he would just lean in and say "head down, wings out, can't fall..." I have long thought on what he really meant. And now as I prepare for the first salvo of this war, I think I understand.

Head down. Many of us try to live with our heads not in the sand. When our heads are down we are eating or looking for something to eat. It is when we are the most likely to be attacked but we have trust, trust in the mob around us.

Wings out. It is not our feathers that steer us. The knowledge that the winds steer us based on the positions of our feathers.

Can't fall. I will admit this took me the longest to figure out but I now understand. Dearest beloved I understand. Faith. Faith in the All Feather. If you have trust in the Mob. If you have the knowledge of our kind and faith in the All Feather, we cannot be defeated.

While I am an old bird by many standards, I feel that I still have a lot to give and I will soon have children. It is up to me to give them something more than what was given to me. The conventional tactic for war is to line up, stand in a mass and one by one have the dominate members charge out and hiss. That is the convention but I will show them something truly different.

If my letters have a pause between them, I am sorry. Do not think that I have fallen, rather that I am so caught up in winning I just do not have time to write.

With all my love,
Edward R Long-toe.

Dear Celene

I find myself lucky and blessed to write to you once more. It is clear the All Feather, for what ever reason, has decided to look out for my well being. I am not so arrogant to think this divine providence is anything to do with my legs but I know in the bottom of my heart it is because of you. My swift love, my feathered beauty, you who stood by me even though the entire courts of the High Mob were insisting that I was in the wrong. Given your families good standing, I believe if you had turned on me like I said you should, I would have been put to death. However, it is clear that you are made of greater substance than I. The All Feather smiled upon us and I live another day. My replacement, who is so young he still has a wonderful pattern to his feathers, took us to the field of battle. A battle field he did not bother scouting or listening to sound advice. William advised him that this was a wonderful battlefield, if he wished to die. I am still perplexed by William. While he is clearly brilliant I have a feeling that he has clearly gone mad. I hear him at night, sitting alone saying a strange word over and over. Hiy..I do not understand its meaning or how he manages to make this sound but night after night.. Hiy, Hiy. Without the burden of command, I went over to his encampment to ask him is there anything I could do to ease his madness. He looked at me and smiled, then looked around conspiratorially and then shared his madness with me. He had found one of those strange Short-neck huts. Within one of these huts he found a small Short-neck. A young one. Newly hatched. I was deep into his madness so I continued to ask. He told me over a number of days he had been eating with this Short-neck and they had been spending some time learning. Many would see this a traitors behaviour but as my father used to say. Any Long- neck that can count above twenty can never be a traitor.

On that fateful day we made our way out upon the battlefield. The fancy feathered commander made us stand in ranks and lower our necks and stomp. The plan was for one by one to go out and fight a single Short-neck. Fine tactics for an honour duel between mobs, utter madness against this enemy. In a mere blink of an eye ten of our mob had fallen. The others frozen in fear. Our fancy feathered leader, like many before him put his head in the sand. Like any good member of the Mob I took command and ordered the Mob into the small groups of three and ordered them to scatter. To the Short-necks I am sure it looked like running around aimlessly. However, I had learnt in our last engagements the Short-necks carry only a certain number of pebbles. Once their strange sticks made that strange sound, we attacked, just like my father taught me. We kicked them to death. Taking the lives of so many Short- necks brings me no joy but it was important that our mob held its shape. We snatched victory out of defeat but it was not enough. We will not win this war in a conventional sense. This is an unconventional war and we need unconventional fighters.

I will continue to fight this war. More and more so...for you and our children.

I remain forever yours,

Edward R Long-toe.

Dearest Mother

Things are becoming more serious out here. I have heard whistles of Long-toe putting together an elite group of outsiders to help in the war effort. This would mean I would no longer be needed here. I beseech you once more, please do what you can to convince father to get me out of here. I grow tired and weary. Not even Cecil's attempt at humour lifts my spirits. I am like a Tunneller in a tree or a Glider in the sunlight. I am out of place.
I pray to the All Feather everyday for my freedom. No one is meant for war, let alone me.

I fervently await your reply, Mother.

Percival Headsand

November 15th, 1932
From William J Whistlebeak
to his wife Maggie

Dearest Maggie

I apologise for my neglect in writing to you. My work has taken over every aspect of my life. I do not wish for you to think that I have forgotten about you. I just never learned to juggle work and life. My mind is both my weakness and my strength. I can only ever focus on one thing and for that I truly am sorry.

You have Edward to thank for this letter. He pulled me aside and reminded me of the importance of family. The ones we are fighting for back at home. He truly is a wise bird. Whether it be reminding those of important things or teaching us to scatter instead of standing still in the line of spitting pebbles, wisdom flows from his beak. He has a head full of knowledge acquired through a lifetime of experience. I hope in time I will learn to think like him. Not wholly, as I do not wish to sacrifice who I am, but with a degree of unity. I am tired of war. There are far more important things than fighting over land and food. The study of said land and food for example. This war, I would argue, is pointless. Although I enjoy studying the Short-necks we would need not be at war to learn of their ways. I would simply approach them, ask them and then spend as much time as possible observing them. They most definitely would agree to that as well. They are a peaceful bunch when they are not trying to kill us. Which makes me think that this is not personal. I could be wrong though.

I digress. I am beginning to bore you with the talk of my work. You can understand why my focus has to be on one thing. For that reason I will end this letter here. I miss you, my wife. Please give the children my regards and thank Henry for his service. Things will return to how they were soon, I am certain of it.

Until I see you, Dear Maggie, know that I am amazed by all you do.

William J Whistlebeak

Dearest Greta

Time moves slower here in the west. It feels like we have been fighting this war for years. Edward keeps telling us to trust in the All Feather to see us through, trust in each other and trust this war will not last. I see my brothers waver from time to time, I can understand why. To be under constant pebble spitting from the enemy can wear a bird down. Some don't sleep as well as they used to. The sound of battle still echo's through their ears. I sat with James this morning. Quite a young bird, barely lost his stripes. He hides his fear well. Barely even bobs his head under pressure. These are the birds to watch out for. They are unpredictable, even to their own. I reminded him of why we fight and encouraged him to not lose his focus and always keep an eye out for the Mob at large. I pray the All Feather will give him a sound mind. We are in a time most father's would never want their sons to live in. All we can do is eat the melon that's in front of us. Life goes on.

Please tell the children I am thinking of them and cannot wait to see them once this war comes to an end.

Yours always,

John Feathers

FINAL EDITION

 THE DAILY MOB

★★ EST 1901   ★★★★★★★★★   ★★16 Nov 1932

LONG-TOE KEEPS HEAD IN THE SAND

Edward Long-toe has had his head buried in the sand since this war began. His decisions have been as erratic as the scattering he has implemented. Many retired mob members who fought in the Great Striper War do not understand this Long-toe method either. "The mob is supposed to move as one." said Theodore Gizzardwing. Despite all the criticism Long-toe has still managed to earn himself a promotion. Many of our fellow mob have been greatly injured in this war and Long-toe is running out of time to fulfil his promise of ending the conflict as quickly as possible. On the night of this paper's release the local mob will be gathering by the lake to drop pebbles into the water in remembrance of those we have lost. All are welcome.

Column by Deidre Gizzardwing

MINI STRIPER FINDS ROCK PILE

Local mini striper Billy came across a strange pile of rocks while foraging for invisible ants late yesterday. Placed neatly on top of one another it is clear that someone or something placed them there. Tracks were found nearby that appeared to be identical to ones that were found near the last location of a recent missing striper. Lawrence Wynd declined to comment but his one raised eyebrow said it all. One theorist believes it to be evidence of Short-necks but most dismiss the claim due to the fact that Short-necks have proven to be extremely noisy in all they do and surely one would have been spotted by now. Billy intends to solve the mystery and has hired a screecher to help map out the area and search for more piles and possible witnesses.

Column by Norman McWhistle

PERSONAL COLUMN

Patricia. I found that thing you were looking for. It was lodged in the tree branch just out of sight. I have no idea how it got there. Do you think Philip might be behind it? Its value is quite high so maybe he wanted to trade it for some food. I can understand that. Slim pickings these days. Let's meet for a drink and I can give you the thing back. My cave is always open, except for late evenings. You understand how things are with my family? I look forward to seeing you. T.

CLASSIFIEDS

Prickle is in need of anyone willing to laugh at his jokes Genuine laughers encouraged to apply. Will be paid in whatever food is favoured. Meeting everyday when the sun is highest under the leaning tree by the water. Predators need not apply

JOKE OF THE DAY

what did the tree hugger say when someone trimmed his claws? Eucalyptus!

Local Bouncers were often used to gather intel from the Short-necks.

Many Bouncers were trained young as they were proven to be the most successful.

Dearest Greta

It amazes me that even in times of war there are moments of peace. A day with no conflict has put the Mob at ease. We spent today feasting on the crops of our enemies. As I tasted the Short-neck's freshly grown barley my thoughts were drawn back home. I rest easy knowing that our children's bellies are full and are the safest they can be. It wasn't that long ago they first hatched and I began teaching them to fend for themselves. I assure you, my dear, we will be a family again soon and I will pass on the knowledge of all I have learned while on the front lines.

I have been reflecting on my chicklinghood. When my brothers and sisters and I would race each other around the water and my father would watch over us, keeping an eye out for the featherless ones and Stripers. We felt free and safe. This is what I want for our children. Current events weigh heavy on me but as I have said many times before, the thought of seeing you once more gives me hope.

There are days I feel like one of our pink and grey cousins. Flying with no real purpose, never paying attention to their surroundings, a fool. But just like everyone else, no one can read the mind of another so the Mob is unaware of how I feel. These days are rare and it doesn't take much for me to shake it off. An encouraging word from Edward, a joke from Cecil or even watching William conduct his research. A glimpse of regular life. The place we all wish to be instead of waging war on the dusty plains on the outskirts of the Short-neck settlements.

In these uncertain times it is best to focus on the things we know. We no longer live in hunger, our families are safe from danger and the Mob is lead by a great bird. The future is in capable wings.

Tell the children I am thinking of them always and remind Joan to be careful of her pebble to food ratio.

Yours always,
John Feathers

November 22nd, 1932
From Percival Headsand to his Mother

Dearest Mother

How many letters must I send you? My writing rivals that of William J Whistlebeak's. Not in quality but in quantity. I will never match the mind of William but that is not important. I do not belong here. How often must I say it before you will send me the help I need?

Percival Headsand

November 22nd, 1932
From William J Whistlebeak
to Henry Hookwing

Dear Henry

I have been pondering on the expedition. Were we sent west for more than food? Did the High Mob know it would lead to war? I am not one for conspiracies but I cannot help but be intrigued. We the Mob have always come together in times of need, without question. It's part of our nature but if we have learned anything from Long-toe's leadership. Sometimes nature can be changed. A Howler lives for the hunt but time spent with a Short-neck will minimise, if not remove, its desire. Just as a screeching cousin can seem perfectly happy behind bars in a Short-neck's dwelling in the place where food is regularly prepared. I know of the dangers in studying the enemy but they are far too interesting to ignore. I would be shaming myself to simply drop everything and focus only on the war itself. However, Long-toe would be very pleased if I did. He talks often of my brilliant mind. His words, not mine. That does not make it any less true though.

How is my Maggie? I am yet to receive any of her letters. Most likely a problem with the postal service or maybe they are hidden beneath the mountain of work I have before me. Either way, tell her I am thinking of her and I hope to hear from her soon.

I have been gathering so much information about the west and those that reside here. The Bouncers here are much like those back home. Some grey, some red, some looking for a fight, others docile. They know the Short-necks well and I have learned much from them.

Time is short Henry, I have fallen behind in my work but I am still motivated to keep going. Once this war is over I shall return home and thank you beak to beak for all you have been doing.

William J Whistlebeak

November 28th, 1932
From William J Whistlebeak
to Henry Hookwing

Dear Henry

I write to remind you of the importance of our work. The world is a different place now, at least out here in the 'land of fruit and caterpillars.' These Short-necks have been relentless with their attacks on us. They threaten more than our lives. They threaten the preservation of our history. I have not stopped working since the beginning of this expedition and it pains me to say that my supplies are now low. I have requested more from Long-toe but he is more preoccupied with current events. Understandable. He has a war to win and his focus must be on accomplishing that, as mine is on gathering knowledge. That hasn't stopped him from roping me into his planning though. Sometimes my mind is a burden.

I have put myself in danger yet again for the sake of my work. To be precise, I met with another Short-neck. The encounter was by chance while mapping out one of the harvesting sites. We both approached slowly and cautiously. The Short-neck stood a toe's length shorter than I and was hiding his nerves poorly. Every time I tilted my head as a greeting he would flinch. Such odd behaviour. Despite the language barrier we made some progress in communicating and I intend to make another attempt again soon. I am still unsure if I should mention this to Edward though I am certain he knows already. I am concerned he will want to take advantage of the situation and use me to acquire information from the enemy. I understand his position but I am reluctant to give up such an incredible chance to understand the Short-neck culture.

The enemy's military is something to be seen. They are creative, or try to be. They have found ways to move their LCM's around so they can go where we go. We still hold the advantage as they struggle to keep up with our movements. I am yet to learn where the Short-necks acquire the golden pebbles they spit at us. I am not the only one that wonders why they do it either. It is true the odd one will hurt us but mostly they just bounce off our bodies. Do they not find it wasteful? Not long ago food was scarce. We struggled to eat and drink. As a species we learnt to always finish what is before us. I think I will try and communicate this to the Short-neck I met with but first I must gain its trust. If I tilt my head less I may just get through the barrier of communication. Time will tell. It has been many months since I left home. I trust you have been well and are taking good care of my Maggie. I look forward to hearing of your exploits back home. I would like to believe things are just as they were when I left but we all know the saying 'The only thing unchanging is the order in which we eat. Food then pebbles. Never pebbles then food'

William J Whistlebeak

Dearest Mother

When I wrote asking for your help I did not expect you to respond so quickly. Nor did I expect you to do the opposite of what I requested. Father arrived recently and has been somewhat overbearing in his support for me. He suddenly wants to see me become a successful soldier. His expectations are too high. He sees my wings and expects me to fly. Does he confuse me with our lying cousins? So perfect in their impersonations. I can flap my wings but I cannot leave the ground. Why does he not understand? This war has broken me. I am not comfortable with the order from General Long-toe to break into smaller mobs in an attempt to confuse the enemy. It is my belief that we are stronger as one. One giant mob. Twenty Twenty and Twenty Twenty strong. The Short- necks would be terrified as there are more of us than them. They would be the ones with their heads in the sand instead of chasing us with their LCM's. Each time they spit their pebbles the sound gets louder. It cannot keep going like this. This war needs to end and soon.

A few times they have tried raising morale with singers and jokers. I could argue of its effectiveness but I am so tired, tired of everything. I have been here so long I have forgotten why we came. Mother, it would mean so much to me if you would write to Father and ask for him to take me home. He will not listen to me. He just keeps encouraging me. He has helped me perfect my scattering and my head tilting which I've heard is an effective tactic for weirding out the Short-necks but I long to be home again. To see my friends and hear you sing those songs to the All Feather. When can things return to the way they were?

Your son,

Percival Headsand

Dearest Celene

I am glad to hear that the home front is going so well. If some Long-neck were to ask me if I had to choose between raising my eggs or leading the Mob to victory, I think it is clear which I would choose.

The High Mob has once again promoted me. While I appreciate their support I am starting to feel their promotions are some what disingenuous. When they promoted me from Colonel to General, in many ways this made sense. It was somewhat odd to be given orders to other Generals of great mobs and telling them our new way to fight. After the battle of the pond on the hill, when I commanded our force to route the entire enemy in one afternoon, the promotion to the new rank of Great Mob General made some kind of sense. I am currently commanding twenty twenty twenty mobs. With so many Generals there needed to be zero doubt who was in command. However, now after my victory at little big tree, being promoted to Supreme Great Mob General is now becoming ridiculous. I almost feel the High Mob is using this war to gain some kind of favour back at home and these promotions do nothing but serve their odd agenda in some way shape or form. Though I pray to the All Feather I never become that cynical.

As I sit here and write to you on the long trail to our next water hole I find my self smiling at the faces around me. Having the gang back together, having Skipper and his odd balls and misfits reminds me of simpler times. Today again Skipper asked me about you and wanted me to remind you it was never to late to sleep with a Red and as always I kicked him in the chest and he had to be carried into battle. I do not understand why he insists in annoying me so. John says it is because I need to let off steam and Skipper knows it. I like

John. While he is barely old enough to ditch his patterns, that is a Long-neck you could trust.

As per your last request from yourself and his wife Greta, I have managed to keep John out of the biggest battles. While he has been made up to Captain and now commands a mob of his own, I have kept them as my aid to camp. This has kept him out of the bulk of the hard fighting. It hurts that I must keep such a promising young bird on the sidelines but I understand why it is important to do so.

As I look around these males it it clear to me, with all the intelligence of William or the good breeding of a Samuel, John is the best of us. From a great and powerful family but unlike the others from great families he was one of the first to volunteer and join me on this expedition. He and his entire family were wealthy enough not to have been bothered by the food crisis and yet he is here. Based on the letters you have sent me it is clear now that a new nation will be born after this war, a nation of laws, a nation where the High Mob do not control the day to day of our every existence. There is one bird that should lead us into this bright new future and that bird is John.

Tomorrow's battle is the most important in the war and John has convinced me to move my camp into the centre to command the battle field more efficiently. While I understand John is just trying to get his mob into the action, after asking and asking I feel I cannot keep him from this battle. Please let his beloved wife know that I will keep him safe. I have assigned the squad to his mob and Skipper will be there to deal such a kicking if anything were to happen to his bird.

With any luck the next time I write it will be with the news that this war will soon be over and I will be coming home.

With all my love,
Edward R Long-toe

My dearest Greta

I pray this letter finds you in good health and I thank the All Feather that you and the children have been safe from this war. The only thing that has gotten me through each day is the thought of returning home to you.

Reinforcements arrived recently and we have proven to be a formidable force. Edward has flown up the ranks and is now General. He remains focused even as he mourns every lost mob under his command. When it comes to a tough decision he still pulls out the shiny pebble that's too big to swallow, stares at it with great focus and always, always makes the right call. The Short-necks have been using methods beyond my comprehension. They have somehow found a way to move at will their LCM's. They can follow us wherever we go. Their numbers are small but they have a knack for putting the fear of the All Feather in us. The reinforcements have boosted our morale and we are all confident under Edwards leadership. Even Percival has turned around. After doing everything he could to be sent home he now embraces the mob life with a fierce confidence. Every soldier has a defining moment. Percy's came when he stared down the enemy and survived the full force of their golden pebbles. If that won't change a bird I don't know what will. A few nights back it was very quiet in regards to the Short-necks so Edward had some entertainment organised. A gal named Betty sung beautifully and a Tree Hugger provided some fantastic comedy. It was the night of peace we needed. It helped me remember what we are fighting for.

Our families and loved ones remain safe and well fed. Now we must work to end this war. I, as always, am convinced this can end in such a way that both sides may benefit. Ultimately, peace between us. There is more I could write but time does not permit. We head out again in the morning on a simple operation that will rattle the Short-necks. Edward has entrusted me with leading a mob and recently promoted me to captain. I will endeavour to lead as he does...with bravery, honour and humility. I love you my dear, Greta. I dream of entangling wings once more and embarrassing the children.

Yours always,

John Feathers

3

THE HOMEFRONT

"I will fly when you cannot, for my victory is your victory"

All Feather

LIFE GOES ON FOR THOSE AT HOME

Many families feel the struggle with their fathers away at war but one young mob have been an encouragement to everyone around them. The Clawtips have been travelling around performing their whistling show leaving everyone in high spirits. The idea came from youngest chick Helen. "I just want to share the comfort I feel when I hear someone whistling." Said Helen. The Clawtips regularly gather by the water to practice their whistling. Many gather with them and are encouraged to join in building a strong community. The Clawtips will be performing at the upcoming talent show hosted by Prickle who promises us guaranteed laughter this time.

Column by Norman McWhistle

CATERPILLARS ARRIVE

Very little caterpillars were found in the land of fruit and caterpillars but that didn't stop the aficionado's from gathering as many as they could find. The privately funded harvesting operation is lead by Joseph T O'Preen who has partnered with the Tunnellers to help with transportation. The first shipment arrived this morning with more expected next week. These caterpillars won't be cheap so you better start saving.

Column by Audrey E Quillington

CREATURE SIGHTED

Something was seen travelling towards the mountains a few nights ago. Witnesses described its movements as sleek and fast. "I have never seen anything like it before." said an anonymous Glider "It was black as night and if not for my ability to see in the dark I may not have noticed it all." The sighting has sparked many a hearty debate and some have put together a hunting party to track it down. "If it's real, we will find it." said Anthony Sniffington. A guarantee from one of the top Howlers.

Column by Arnold Sly

— PERSONAL COLUMN —

Mary. I thought now would be the best time to confess my undying love for watermelon. Its insides require very little pebbles to grind up and its seeds are fun to spit at annoying neighbours. The first time I tried watermelon I wasn't so sure I'd like it. Do you remember the day we were sitting near the giant rock and one just rolled by? We followed it curiously until it cracked on the base of a tree. We ate every piece of it in one go. I think of that day often. Mmmmm

November 7th, 1932
From Greta Feathers to her husband John

Dearest husband

I received all your letters and have been reading them with the children each night before they sleep. Our youngest Howard has taken it upon himself to organise them into piles and is showing signs of following in your footsteps. He and his brothers have been practicing their scattering down by the empty lakes. They long to impress you and speak of you often.

I am sorry it has been so long since I have written and I fear you might worry that I have forgotten you but truth be the opposite. You are always on my mind and your name is always on my beak. I do not blame you for leaving on the expedition as I know the kind of bird you are but I do wish you would have taken the time to recognise the position our family holds amongst the mobs. We have more than enough food to see us through the drought. There was no need to put yourself in harms way when there are so many others who could have taken your place. It is true no one expected war to come of this but I cannot help but wonder if things would be different if the expedition was half the size. I am not a military leader so it is possible the end result would much be the same. Since so many are away in the war we have been offered free Bouncers to help protect our homes from the featherless ones. Our friend Harriet came close to having an egg stolen but the theft was luckily intervened. We are all working hard to preserve our home and pray to the All Feather that we will have the strength to continue. We hold regular meetings to discuss and plan ways to improve the mobs here so our soldiers will feel celebrated upon their return.

I am happy to see how focused you are and certain of your responsibilities as one of the mob scattering for the freedoms of many but I ask you to remember those you left at home. The children and I love reading your letters so please write as often as you can. We miss you.

May the All Feather guide and protect you.

Greta Feathers

November 12th, 1932
  From Maggie R Whistlebeak to her husband
William

Dear William

I pray the All Feather has kept you safe during this war. I miss you dearly and write to you almost everyday. Although your lack of response makes me uneasy I do understand the importance of your work and the expedition you have undertaken.

Henry has been keeping me up to date with all the news but I would much rather hear it straight from you. These Short-necks sound dangerous but I know your curiosity will get the better of you. Please be careful when you make contact with them and remember you have a family waiting for you at home.

You will be glad to know how well Henry has been looking after me. He sees to posting my letters and has sent our Bouncer to someone who needs the protection more than we do. I have seen Henry stomp one of our 'highest soaring cousins of the sky' as it swooped down to steal a neighbours egg. It reminded me of the time you stood up to the featherless ones when they asked us if we had an egg to spare. You replied with a swift kick. I think of those simpler times often, when you weren't buried in so much work. I can still hear you whistling gently as you lead our children to the fruit trees and showed them how to pick the perfect meal. How excited you were to find the odd caterpillar and cheekily eating one without the children noticing. Will we ever return to those times? Perhaps when the war has ended.

I have heard of the tragic loss of lives but I wonder how the enemy has not suffered a single casualty. Do we have a higher regard of life than they? I do not pretend to understand the mind of soldiers but I do feel our kind has long stopped burying our heads in the sand and moved forward with a readiness to solve any situation that faces us. We are indeed better than we once were as a nation.

I look forward to hearing of your findings when you begin communicating with these Short-necks.

I wait with bated breath to hear from you, dear husband. I will write again soon and pray you will too. Work is important but so is family, never forget that.

Maggie R Whistlebeak

November, 19th 1932
From Celene Long-toe
to her husband Edward

Dearest Edward

I am so very proud of you and all you have accomplished throughout the expedition and now with leading the mobs against those who disregard our right to live. When the incident with the pebbles occurred it shook us both but we remembered what the All Feather said 'I will fly when you cannot, for my victory is your victory.'

We survived the accusations and the gossip and we will get through this war just the same. You are a great leader. Whether it be commanding the mobs or rotating our future children. I will say it once more. I am proud of you, my dear husband.

With every turn of an egg I think of you and the life we are building together as a family. Do not let that thought slip your mind every time you hold the item I gave you. It is my hope that it will keep you grounded as those around you tend to elevate you in a similar light as our cousins of the sky.

Life at home is busy. Even more so since the war began. Mother Maggie spends most her time writing letters to William while Henry helps out with various chores. I am curious to know why father trusts Henry so much. He behaves oddly around her and I am somewhat concerned. I would ask you not to mention this to Father in the off chance that it would hinder his work. Some things are worth sitting on when so much is happening at once. Each problem must be solved one at a time and from most important to least and ending the war is by far the most important.

It is difficult to believe that food was once so scarce. Our bellies are so full of western delicacies we have already forgotten what it was like to be hungry. I hope you are aware of how grateful everyone is of the mobs you lead and all they do. We pray to the All Feather that there will be no more loss of life. Win this war, Edward. Unite the Mobs and return home safely.

Celene Long-toe

November 21st, 1932
From George Lyre
Founder and CEO of the Daily Mob
To the Mobs out west.

I send this letter on behalf of those who continue to live in safety because of your sacrifice.

This war is like a prickly anteater, soft on one side, deadly on the other but one cannot exist without the other.

As you sit in quiet contemplation for the customary twenty minutes before you sleep each night, know that we at home are doing the same. Although our days are different we live under the same sky. Our thoughts are of you as your thoughts are of us.

As we receive word of your accomplishments, we cheer. When we hear of your losses, we mourn. Those here at home may not be in the fight but we stand firmly with you. The young ones are often seen practicing their scattering in pairs. They look up to you and wait in great anticipation for your safe return. These are the ones you are fighting for, never forget that.

May the All Feather give you strength to carry on until the end.

Please enjoy the accompanied gift of the very finest pebbles, courtesy of The Daily Mob.

George Lyre

November 22nd, 1932
From Greta Feathers to her husband John

Dearest husband

As I write this letter, clouds build overhead. Many of us have been tempted to follow where they lead but are constantly reminded that if we were to, we would end up fighting alongside you. As much as I long to see you once again, I am not one to get my wings dirty. That is what the Mob is for but you are aware of this. I pray these words do not come across in an aggressive tone, it is not my intent to be so blunt but this war is unsettling, like a Screamer in the night. The sooner it is over the better.

The children miss you dearly, as do I. We grow ever so accustomed to this new way of life. Our ancestors were never truly one. Only coming together in times of great need and then as sure as the sun, splitting off into pairs when it is all done. Somehow it feels different. As if once the war has ended we will remain as one still. As long as we keep our place amongst the Mob I will be happy. Our children will have the very best as will their children.

John. I am ever so proud of you. Even though we disagree on things we both recognise what is important. We both long to see our kind flourish. We both long for an abundance of fruit and caterpillars for our families. Things seem to be moving that way already so I beseech you once more. Come home as soon as you are able. Your family need you here.

Yours always,

Greta Feathers

November 26th, 1932
From Maggie R Whistlebeak
to her husband William

Dear William

If words could fully describe my feelings at this moment I would never put down the quill. Your silence is deafening. I understand your work is extremely important but I wish you would write home, if only one line to let us know we are on your mind.

If I could acquire the help of a hundred Tunnellers I would have them dig a path to you while remaining safe from the war.

I am sorry for my emotional state. I walked by the broken rock with Henry today and I was reminded of the day we met, when we both were chasing watermelons and enjoyed a hearty meal after they broke into pieces as they collided. I will never forget that day. If only we could return there and start our lives over. I miss the simpler times.

I am tired of this war, tired of worrying about you and tired of the state of the land. My Dear William, what will it take for things to return to the way they were? If you have a moment, maybe you could put some time into researching possible ways for us to start over. I still have much hope left in me. Although this letter is short and some might say confusing, it is one I needed to write, if not for myself. I need you, William. I am doing my best without you but feel like I am falling short. I never felt this way until you left on your expedition. Maybe I should start an expedition of my own, for I am in search of as many answers as you, only I know where to find them. You, however, tend to take the long way round.

May the All Feather give you wisdom, my husband.

Maggie R Whistlebeak

November 26th, 1932
From Celene Long-toe
to her husband Edward

Dearest Edward

I am disheartened to hear how often High Command has messed you around. Why would they put you in charge if they believe you are incompetent? I will never understand the way their minds work. They sit up there on their pebble filled mountain not knowing what it is like for us everyday birds below. You are a far better bird than they are, Edward, never forget that. You are surrounded by those who both admire and respect you.

I have been collecting all the news articles that mention you and reading them to our unhatched children. They are close now, I can feel it. There are moments where I struggle as I wish you were here to imprint on them as they take their first steps. Is it possible that the war would be over by then? We can only hope.

Keep your eyes on where we are heading, my husband. Think of your family but also our nation. I kid myself. Here I am encouraging you to do things you already do. I guess that is the best I can do. Remind you of who you are and how far you have come. We have been through so much together and never have wavered in our devotion to one another. The distance between us is just another test for us and I am certain it will strengthen us. As I hold onto the hope of reuniting soon, I pray to the All Feather that he will keep you safe until that time.

I am proud of you, Edward, forever and always.

Celene Long-toe

4

ORDERS FROM COMMAND

"Yes sir!"

All the soldiers

November 1st, 1932
From the from the desk of High Command
Dictated by Cleary Feathers

To Lieutenant Edward R Long-toe and for his eyes alone.

I have received your last communication and to say I am disappointed is an understatement. We have given you command of a single mob which by my considerable calculation is more than enough. To ask for twenty twenty mobs is the definition of madness.

Based on the detailed information you have provided, which might I add took three of the laughing brothers and sisters to deliver. We have determined that this meeting will be the first step to an amazing peace between the two nations.

It would appear based on the food and the region there is more than enough space for our two great nations. Based on the very detailed review you have provided it is clear that we are the superior species. We can run very fast for a short distance and while waving our wings around. Based on your description these Short-necks drip water from their featherless bodies when they run...Truly baffling.

I look forward to hearing about your success in the peace negotiation and would expecting nothing less than twenty twenty twenty twenty twenty of the food and land.

November 6th, 1932
  From the from the desk of High Command
  Dictated by Cleary Feathers

To Junior officer Edward R Long-toe and for his eyes alone.

Despite my best efforts and long pleading for you to consider the risk it
appears that we are now undoubtably at war.

Had you provided more detailed information I would have recommended you
bring at least Twenty Twenty mobs with you to this peace summit. Because of
this, the deaths of our brothers are on you.

I am sending someone to relieve you of command, my very own son in fact.
While he may only be out of his fluff he will be a far better commander than
you ever were.

When it comes to command and leadership....Breeding matters, not
experience.

November 16th, 1932
  From the desk of the High Command
  Dictated by Cleary Feathers

To Captain Edward R Long-toe and for his eyes alone.

When it comes to battle, experience is key, I would be remiss if I left it unsaid about apologies. Due to my own arrogance my son is dead. Due to your skill, knowledge and will...the mobs under your command are alive....

I wish for you to move forward and engage the enemy, but only if you are certain of victory. If you are not certain pull back...but do not pull back if that means defeat..

November 27th, 1932
  From the desk of the High Command
  Dictated by Cleary Feathers

To General Edward R Long-toe and for his eyes only.

While I remain unimpressed with your current efforts in leading us towards victory I am still pressured by many to promote you even further. At this current time I have made the decision to turn down the everyday mob's request for yet another promotion and leave you at your current post. You fed our nation General Long-toe, now end this war and earn another promotion.

5

JOURNAL ENTRIES

"Thoughts. They are wonderful are they not?"

William J Whistlebeak

— (DUE TO THE STATE THESE
JOURNALS WERE FOUND IN,
TRANSLATION WAS DIFFICULT
AND AS A RESULT DATES ARE
ABSENT.)

From the diary of Edward R Long-toe

The first attack

Dear diary

The day started with the coldest fog rolling across our chosen battle field.
While the rest of my twenty suggested we wait for a more clear morning,
William suggested this was the perfect time for my plan. He still considered
my plan insane but isn't that what we all said about the land of fruit and
caterpillars? I gave the signal and as planned the mob scattered in all
directions. The freedom. No more ridged formations. No more standing while
the Short-necks spit their pebbles at us...After twenty units of passing time,
the field was ours and the day was won.

The replacement

Dear diary

It appears that I have been left out here to die. Not a death by pebble or by
kick, by shame. They have sent a young bird to replace me. To think that after
my many victories. I am to be replaced by a bird so young his stripes are yet
to fade. He has decided the best strategy is to challenge the enemy...one on
one..I fear I will not live out the rest of the year.

The item

Dear diary

Everyday I look upon the item given to me by Celene. One that reminds me of home, Celene and all that I fight for. I feel there is a connection between it and our enemy. The weapons they use are made of a similar material. If only their tactics were as good as their craftsmanship then they wouldn't be struggling so hard to defeat us.

Tactics

Dear Diary

I have found scattering is the most promising tactic to assure our survival. I have split the Mob into smaller groups and appointed the tallest of us as lookouts. This has proven effective in confusing the Short-necks. William offers up his own ideas on occasion but I suspect it is only because he feels obligated to. His mind is always drifting to his work. I pray to the All Feather that his mind may drift back to the importance of winning this war. A mind like his is priceless.

Short-neck second attempt

Dear diary

The sun pierced through my feathers as it reached its peak of the day. Dust rolled towards us with a loud hum. Emerging from the cloud of dust came the Short-necks. They devised a way to move around with their LCM's. With so many targets to choose from the enemy were unable to overwhelm us with sheer force. Another battle won with very little casualties.

A temporary set back

Dear diary

Our overconfidence lead to a lapse in judgment that cost the lives of some of the Mob. This war weighs heavy on our souls but the All Feather will see us through. I have ordered some of the troops to regroup so we can change our strategy. We will win the day and we will win the war for the sake of our children.

The squad

Dear diary

I never thought I would be calling on the crew once more but it seems I have no choice. I have exhausted all options and I will need to do this once more it would seem. I approached them individually and they all accepted. Some were a bit more hesitant than others but what matters is they are back at it again. The unlikely group of outsiders. A Striper, a Tree Hugger, a Bouncer and a Tunneller. Like a joke waiting for a punchline the enemy won't be laughing at.

Morale

Dear diary

I can feel a shift in the morale of the Mob. They are weary of the fight. Bellies full of grain bring temporary joy but they cannot hide their longing to return home. I have written and rewritten the plans for our next attack. I wish to end this war like I promised in the beginning. Quickly. Until we head out for the attack, I must find a way to raise morale. All Feather knows we need it.

John

Dear diary

John Feathers has proven to be an outstanding soldier. His optimism and encouragement for others is what spurs a lot of us on. Constantly reminding us of what we fight for. I believe he is ready for his own command and I am certain he will accept the offer with open wings but doing so will break the promise I made to his family to keep him out of the frontlines. But what if placing him there will win us the war?

Success

Dear diary

Everything is falling into place. We have had a series of successful operations and have completely rattled the Short-necks. The outsiders I brought in have played their part perfectly. Despite their sometimes rogue behaviour, especially Skipper, for the better part they have followed my orders to the letter. At last the end is in sight.

One last push

Dear diary

Everything we have worked for has come to this moment. The enemy have become tired and agitated. We have worn them down. Our victory is inevitable. I pray to the All Feather that all will happen with minimal casualties. The Mob have unanimously declared their willingness to give their lives for our freedom but I am not one to sacrifice them without care nor thought. If John and the team of outsiders are successful in their mission we will all make it out with barely a scrape.

The Future

Dear Diary

I spent today pondering on where we are headed as a mob, as a nation. We once lived separately. Only ever coming together for the important things. We were lead by fools. We still are. Change is something that is needed for us to prosper. Gathering together should be done for more than just food. We should debate the tough topics, make the tough decisions all while thinking about our unhatched chicks and their unhatched chicks. More alliances need to be made. I have laid the foundations with the squad of outsiders but more work needs to be done. I can see it now. A nation built on freedom and liberty. One mob under All Feather, united in our common interests. I fear this burden will ultimately be left to me. If I can just convince William to put his research on hold and help build a strong nation of free birds, it may just be our greatest achievement. By no means will I ask him to throw away his life's work. On the contrary, I will encourage him to finish it but first remind him that not all work needs to be done alone.

On this day the words of my father ring true. He often said 'a bird is more than its feathers.' As I look upon the mob I have lead in this war, each soldier has an important part to play. It is not their feathers that give them strength to fight. It is not their feet nor their wings. It is their spirit. Their heart. And that is why we will win this war. My dear friend John often reminds me of the value of freedom. It emerges from the egg when we hatch and it is something we must fight for. Preserve. And although this war is more about our right to live than anything else, it must never leave our hearts and minds. For if we only focus on one thing, we risk losing what we take for granted. Freedom.

From the diary of William J Whistlebeak

War

War is a funny thing. Not in the way of our laughing cousins, as I would never find death amusing. By funny, I mean strange. Strange how everyone responds so differently. Some panic. Some plant their toes firmly on the ground. Some believe they can join our cousins in the sky. I for one do none of that. I stand back and take it all in. Study things carefully. From time to time I will give Long-toe my advice and I am surprised as to how often he will listen. Part of me wants this war to carry on for a little longer. I am beginning to understand the enemy but to fully understand their tactics and how their minds work, I will need more time.

Interaction

I have made contact with another Short-neck civilian. Female. At least half my height. She appears unafraid but still remains cautious. She offered me food. Seeds to be exact. A delicacy back home. I may have offended her by taking her entire supply in one snap of the beak. I will learn more in the upcoming days. I am still undecided on reporting my research to Edward. I know he is trustworthy but I also know the bird he is.

Short-necks

These Short-necks are not too different from the Mob in a few small ways. They sleep far away from each other but come together when food is involved. Their food, however, is surrounded by dead trees and a cold sharp vine. Such odd behaviour.

Short-neck military

With every conflict we have I grow closer to understanding the enemy but sometimes I think my intelligence is being diminished by the sheer insanity of the methods these Short-necks go to. Despite the minimal effectiveness of the pebbles they spit at us in great volume, they somehow believe it will eventually work. They have now developed a way to move these laughing cousin mimics around at will. This method fails as they cannot match our speed and one would think they are aiming for our cousins in the sky instead. This really does leave me baffled.

Thoughts from the outside

I spent some time today conversing with those who have been looking in from the outside of this conflict. The local bouncers act like nothing is happening. They are completely disinterested. The featherless ones watch from a distance, hoping to pick off the injured. I am yet to approach one of them because the blood in the air tends to aggravate them. The screechers have a lot to say though. They believe Long-toe should change his entire strategy. Instead of scattering we should dance. I do not see that working in any scenario, regardless of the magnitude of the threat. The Tunnellers think our best bet would be attacking from underneath but failed to offer their services. Everyone has their ideas but not many follow them to their logical conclusions.

Further on

I have travelled as far as permitted by the High Mob and Long-toe but I am curious. The air is different out here. There is a certain smell I cannot place. A smell I am compelled to find the source of. There are stories of an endless lake you cannot drink from. This could be it but there is no way of verifying it unless I can travel further on. Perhaps when the war ends I will see it for myself. Perhaps I will find another way before then.

Robert

I have been meeting with another Short-neck regularly. We have begun breaking through the language barrier. Short-neck is not a term they understand nor like. The preferred term is Robert. He said this while pointing at himself. Despite trying to clarify my own name he now calls me Ee-moo. It is a little condescending if you ask me. I will work on better ways to communicate and hopefully this Robert will start using a different method other than food. Not that I am complaining.

The latest skirmish

I am pleased to be partaking in very little battles in this war. I watch from a distance and help with tactics as Long-toe understands the importance of my work. This latest skirmish was not pretty. The Mob was delayed for mere moments and it cost us lives. If I have learnt anything from working with Edward Long- toe it is, in war there must be precision. The look outs must not blink and always be watching. I am sure they will not make this mistake again.

Home

Home is something I do not think of as much as I should. My assistant Henry is someone I find myself trusting with protecting my wife and family back home. He was first part of the twenty twenty mob heading out west but then suddenly requested to stay behind. I was first confused but then begun to understand the benefits of such action. My Maggie is an attractive bird that many wish to call their own. Henry's strong presence will keep those bothersome males away and from what I have heard thus far, it has worked.

Anthropology

Anthropology. The study of Short-neck societies. This will be a lifetime commitment. One I am ready to take on with extreme focus. I worry, however, that my work will one day be used against the Short-necks for nothing but ill reasons. There is always an agenda, good or bad, but I mostly worry about the bad. The Tree Hugger for example. Sleeping is their primary aim. Everything they do is to arrive at that goal. Long-toe's agenda is to win this war so we can all go home but the High Mob may have a conflicting agenda of their own. It is endless. As I study these Short-Necks I will be cautious with what i choose to reveal and to whom.

Short-neck shelters

I have been watching theses Short-necks closely. One thing I find intriguing are their shelters. As darkness begins to fall they go inside and prevent anything from entering. Somehow they create their own light from within. I have peered through the cracks of these shelters and seen how bright it is inside. I often wonder as I peer in, can they see me as they peer out? I am uncertain of this. They behave like someone who has seen something but aren't willing to share that with anyone, even the one they are staring at. I have a lot of questions that need answering. I hope to meet with a Robert again soon and continue learning.

Eyes are watching

I have begun being more cautious than usual. I feel like someone is watching me. It was only a matter of time before someone noticed my regular disappearances. Studying the Short-necks up close may have to be set aside for the time being. My focus now will be on our interactions through the war.

Thoughts

As I look around at the Mob settling down to sleep. Some write letters while others quietly whistle. It is hard to read their thoughts. They sit calmly as if they have already forgotten the events of the day. Long-toe still spends his time looking at the shiny pebble too large to swallow. What thoughts scatter through his mind? It is in those times the ability to read minds would be desirable. The only mind I believe I can read with precision are the featherless ones... or the Tunnellers that only care about digging and sometimes charging at those who annoy them.

Anticipation

Changing my focus has proven to be more difficult than I first anticipated. I think back to the Robert i was meeting with. He liked to run his fingers down my neck. Such odd behaviour. Roberts like to touch everything they can. Some have befriended howlers and regularly rub their bellies. An act that appears well received. This act is something I wish to learn more about. What is their reason for it? Do they expect all creatures to expose their bellies and receive such rubs?

Victory in sight

Edward R Long-toe has changed ranks so often we are corrected almost everyday. At least the war has an end in sight. I have been advising Edward on many of his operations and if I am honest, I grow tired. I am not meant for war. Indeed I am more than capable of it but my interests lie elsewhere. Not just with my study of the Short-necks but other mysteries like the Striper Killer or how our kind are unable to fly despite having wings like all our cousins. I will find these answers in due time but for now I must help with ending this war. There are far too many distractions because of it.

Thoughts on the future

As the end of the war becomes ever so close I do hope that the Short-necks will not be hesitant to communicate with me. I wish for peace between our nations, a sentiment I am not alone in. I have seen them communicate with many other creatures but they do not look upon them the way they look upon us. Trust is something I will have to earn before I can truly bury my head in the sand of my in depth anthropologic study. I get the sense that they are embarrassed by their choice of tactics in this war. I wonder if in time they will forget this whole ordeal and live peacefully along side us.

From the Diary of John Feathers

Thoughts

Since the war begun we have all been encouraged to write in journals. I find this to be odd behaviour for a mob but Edward has a way of bringing us out of the norms of our society. There was a time when we only ever travelled in pairs but now a mob of twenty and twenty stand together to fight against those who wish to end our lives. And for what? Being hungry? Wanting to feed our families? Is that a crime? The enemy seems to think so.

Greta

I find myself writing letters to Greta more than writing in this journal, or at least thinking about writing to her. My words escape me whenever I pick up the quill. Our disagreements weigh heavy on both of us and this war is not helping. Being so far away makes it more than difficult to work through our problems. I pray to the All Feather that this war may end as fast as it began.

Edward R Long-toe

Our fearless leader has been under a lot of scrutiny from the High Mob. First he is promoted then demoted and promoted once more. They cannot make up their minds. The soldiers see it differently. They know he is best qualified to lead us. Some even say he is over qualified. He has great instincts. While the High Mob would expect us to line up and hold our form, Long-toe says the opposite. His decision for us to scatter saved lives. If only those sceptical could see it. I am proud to call him friend.

Short-necks

There are times I do not understand the enemy. The tactics they adopt with the intent to wipe us from existence baffle me. The golden sharp pebbles they spit at us with great velocity do very little to injure us, however, the quantity sometimes seem to work. I believe their persistence will not bring them victory. We are simply too fast, too wise and too focused. We are forever protected by the All Feather.

William

William is remarkable. We all think that. Counting is his forte yet he rarely ever mentions it. "There are more important things than counting" he often says. He wishes to understand the enemy on a cultural level. He does not care for war and tries to avoid all conversation of it. It is quite amusing watching him sit amongst a group of soldiers and attempt to turn the chatter away from war. It always circles right back.

Freedom

I have been thinking about what it is we are fighting for. It is more than our children. It is more than our right to eat, more than our right to drink, more than our right to survive. It is our right to listen to our instincts or ignore them, to travel the land without threat of being erased from existence. To sit in the shade as tree huggers sleep above. To converse with all creatures or challenge them in friendly combat. It is our right to live! It is Freedom! We fight to be free once more. Free to make choices no matter the outcome. It is our right given by the All Feather. Every action has consequences, good and bad. How else does one learn if not through experience? Life is big. Life is beautiful. This is what we fight for. Life.

Children

I miss my home. I miss my children. I trust Greta has everything in wing. She can be stubborn at times and set in her ways but she loves our children and always does what is best for them. I have received word of them practicing scattering. It seems Long-toe's tactics have reached the Mob back home. I just pray to the All Feather my children will never have to take part in this war or another.

War effort

We have been working tirelessly to bring this war to an end. Edward has broken down the Mob into smaller numbers with taller lookouts and positioned them all through the west. He has approached me for a special operation. Low risk, high reward and if all goes well it could bring about the end of the war for good. Am I ready to lead my own Mob? Am I able? There are times I doubt myself and others I believe I can join our cousins in the sky. If this truly can bring an end to the war, then for the sake of my children...I have no choice.

From the Diary of Percy Headsand

Why?

We were given these journals with the purpose to write in at least once a day.
Apparently it will help with our morale but I do not believe that for one
second. Honestly, I don't have the time nor the motivation for this.

Mother

I have written so many letters home and still Mother ignores my wishes. I am
a bird of many talents and war is not one of them. Well, I could be great at
war but I would rather be home helping those in need. If I recall correctly
someone is planning to start their own pebble business. I could be of great
assistance to them. No one understands pebbles like I do. Why can't Mother
see that? I will write another letter shortly. Surely she will help eventually.

Cecil

Since meeting Cecil I have found his attempt at humour somewhat
unpleasant. We are not a funny species, at least not to us. His jokes fall flat
like a Tree Hugger forgetting to hold onto a branch. Though that is something
I do find amusing. It seems he only has different variations of the same joke.
"Why did the mob travel west? To get to the land of fruit and caterpillars" It
is almost always an exact retelling every time. He's a nice enough bird with a
comically large wingspan . Maybe that's why he gets so many laughs?

Invincible

I have given up on writing in this journal. I pretend to do it from time to time
but nothing has been worth mentioning until now. Today I stood in front of
the enemy as they spat their golden pebbles at the Mob. I thought it was over

for me...but when the noise stopped and the smoke cleared...I was unharmed.

This was a sign from the All Feather. I am meant for great things. Father agrees. Since he joined me in the war we have set aside our differences and both made the decision of focusing on what is important, what is bigger than ourselves. Ending the war.

From the Diary of Reginald Skipper
(The Roo-cruit)

I'm just an old Bouncer and I have the scars to prove it. They say the older
we get the more easy it becomes to fight..to kill. I think as we get older we
hold on to life just a little bit harder and will do anything for just one more
breath each day.

I was young when I joined the Bouncer Corp. I was barely out of the pouch
when I enlisted. I was told that it was the duty of us Reds to ensure that the
Greys understood their place. Three Grey uprisings later and I was singled
out for special training. Much like all my life I was not told what I was
training for. They say I could have been a great prize fighter. That I had quick
hands. Hands never played into fighting Greys though and we were not
fighting Greys...we were fighting fanged devils! What's worse, our trainer
wasn't even a Red! Of all things, one of those damned Long-necks. What
would he know about war and fighting?! Could he even kick?! Well, when I
woke up after he kicked me dead in the chest I thought..perhaps this was a
bird I could follow into war.

We entered that war as optimists, dreaming of a better world with hope for
this alliance. I even started to call that Long-neck... friend.

I was at my normal watering hole, drinking a nice cold one and kicking some
Greys when I heard the sound of the unmistakable walk of that long toed fool.
Through out the war, Edward would get that look in his eyes... purpose.
Before he could even speak I told him that I was retired. Retired from the
Corp, from the alliance..from all the bull! He stood there, waited and before
he could launch into his speech I got up, ready to stand on my tail. He spoke,
telling me of this new enemy and how it was a threat to us all. I told him I
didn't care! He then reminded me of a promise I made to him...for all the

damn things...a promise made in the heat of war..is unbreakable. I agreed to join his little war but I won't be fighting it with long- necks. It was time I called on the alliance, time I got the squad back into hell!

From the diary of Doug McHole
(The Tunneller)

I'm an expert in digging. Done it all my life. My da taught me just like his da taught him. My great da even dug a trap for one of those pesky short-necks years back. It's funny. They have been around far longer than Edward and his mob realises. They just seem to stick to the waters edge is all.

After all this time, Edward came to see me. Said he wanted to put the crew back together. Must be desperate to call on me. He doesn't want his war to drag on too long. The way he described these short-necks and their tactics I am certain I can be of service. It won't be the first time i've messed with their operations. I remember once they hit me with so much force it stopped them in their tracks. I walked it off, they didn't.

Most folks would never be so keen to jump into a war that doesn't effect them in any way but honestly, I think i've missed it. I find more purpose in destruction. Digging homes might seem like an honourable thing but i want something more. To see the frustration on the enemies faces. Realising their failure. It warms my heart.

Edward's offer was easy to accept. Consider me back in the business.

From the diary of Dropper
(The Tree Hugger)

I was awoken from my second daily nap by a familiar beak. Long- toe. I swore I was in my tree when I dozed off. Nevertheless, he found me on the ground. Head pounding. I needed some more leaves but Long-toe was in the way so I had to hear him out. Before I knew it I was agreeing to help him win his war. Gathering intel, distracting the enemy, you know, the kind of things I used to do when the squad was together. Looks like McHole, Skipper, Lightstep and Dropper were going to be back at it again. The unlikely bunch of outsiders working with the Mob. It's unheard of. Maybe that's why we work so well? Those Short-necks won't see us coming. If they do, they won't think anything of it until it is too late.

To me it is odd hearing Edward and his kind calling their enemy Short-necks. Their necks are longer than mine. What do they call me? No neck? Never really understood their way of thinking but if Edward is still paying in leaves he can call me whatever he wants.

I've seen a few Short-necks in my time. Seen 'em walking. Kicking the dirt. Rolling out some sort of shelter and sleeping inside. Seen 'em using old leaves to start a fire. Those leaves could have still been good but what would you expect from a bunch of selfish bastards?! You know I wouldn't put it passed 'em to break a branch and try feedin' me my own leaves but that would just make me not trust 'em even more. Like my Mother always said "Never eat leaves that aren't on the branch. They could be poisoned." Good advice.

I'll admit. The squad back together again. I'm looking forward to it.

From the Diary of Lyle Lightstep (The Striper)

Never seen, never heard. Yet that didn't stop Edward Long-toe from tracking me down. I'm a curious kind. I guess that's why it was so easy for me to fight alongside my food. I'd be lying if I said I hadn't thought about having a nibble on the old squad. Long-toe would know this so he must be desperate to contact me.

I was working with a Howler. Helping hunt down those who are hunting my kind when Long-toe caught up with me. He's a wordsmith. If he wasn't, I wouldn't have abandoned my mission of saving my kind from extinction. I hope my decision doesn't come back to haunt me. Funny that. I'm usually the one doing the haunting. Sleep all day, hunt all night. It's what I was born to do. This new enemy of Long-toe's needs some scaring. I know their scent..and soon I'll know their fears. I like a challenge but this will be a walk through the plains.

Way out west. Far from my home. It will be a long journey to the frontlines. I have told Long-toe to he will need to have someone guarding them at night. There are times I can't control the lust for blood. My instincts are raw and unpredictable. His best bet would be recruiting one of those blue cousins of theirs. The ones with the thin flat thins on their heads. Those things make me uncomfortable. Probably the only thing that does. Maybe one day I will have the privilege of hunting one down but first I will need to get this war out of the way. Long-toe is pretty precise with the particulars. I won't let him down, not this time. And hopefully he will honour the agreement we made the first time he recruited me. He's trustworthy, anyone that has crossed paths with him knows

this. In the end, that's what matters.

6

_____

PEACE

"No matter the length of one's neck, we all long for the same thing."

Edward R Long-toe

SHORT-NECKS SURRENDER TO THE MOB

It may not have happened as quick as we had hoped but peace is finally here. In a surprising move from the relentless Short-necks they finally ceased spitting pebbles at the mob. Not only that, they have relinquished their weapons and acknowledged their defeat. . "The Great Emu War has finally come to an end." said General Longtoe in a recent public address "we scatter no more and once again return to our pair to pair lives." We celebrate with Long-toe and the victors and wait in great anticipation as they make their way back home

Many of the mob and even our allies have begun planning the greatest celebration in the history of the Mob. James O'Preen has been put in charge of catering for the event and has promised many a fruit and caterpillar,

especially watermelons as requested by a very persistent member of the mob. As our lives return to something that resembles normal we remember those we have lost and give thanks to the All Feather for our victory. May the Mob know peace for the rest of time and May we never forget what was accomplished here.

Column by
Norman Mcwhistle

FIRST ANNUAL SCREECHER DANCE PARTY

We always see our screeching cousins of the sky flying But rarely do we ever see them dancing. That is why they have decided to share with the rest of us the one thing that they have kept to themselves since the dawn of time. "We collectively believe Erchh that it is time for us to Erchh share our culture with the rest of our feathered friends but also our featherless ones too." Said Betty Wingjig in her first interview with the Daily Mob "It is our hope Erchh that this will unite us all Erchh in a time when unity is needed." The
dance will not be choreographed in anyway as everyone is encouraged to express themselves in whichever way they wish. Our screeching cousins aren't the only ones celebrating freedom. The Mob too is looking forward to the celebrations.

Column by Audrey E Quillington

PERSONAL COLUMN

George. I would be remiss if I didn't take the time to mention what happened. As you know many of our cousins like to sing but WE do not. We whistle, and I am sure you can imagine what would happen if we ever abandoned the whistle and tried to join in with our cousins. By the All Feather you should have seen it! You have heard the expression 'how does one clear a grazing plain? Let a long-neck sing.' Well, I have seen the results first wing. Please don't sing anymore, George

December 10th, 1932
From Percival Headsand to his Mother

Dearest Mother

The war has ended. Father and I will be returning to you within the month.
The Short-necks retreated earlier today and we are certain of their surrender.
It has been an honour serving under General R Long-toe and fighting
alongside Father. It may sound macabre but this war has been a blessing from
the All Feather. As the saying goes 'where clouds build, water will follow.' I
now understand why I was sent on the expedition and why you sent Father to
war with me. I no longer have my head in the sand and I have you to thank. I
will not bore you with stories from the plains other than the extraordinary
ability I did not know I had. When I heard the sound of the LCM's spitting
their golden pebbles towards us...I cannot explain why or what came over me
but I found myself standing in front of the Mob and taking all of the blast.
When the smoke cleared I stood unharmed while the enemy stood confused.
The All Feather really does watch over us. I have mentioned to Father of my
plan to live in the west permanently. It is something we can discuss on my
return. The future is looking bright, Mother. I will see you soon.
Percival Headsand

Dear Henry

The war may be over but my work has only just begun. I have planned out an extensive anthropologic study into the life and behaviour of Short-necks. During my interactions with one I have learned that the scientific term for their species is Robert. I am uncertain of its origin but given more time my knowledge and understanding will no doubt increase.

I write to you amidst the celebrations. Our glorious leader General Long-toe is being hailed as the greatest leader in the history of the Mob. Not one has spoken ill of him, nor will they. He found food for our starving nation, organised its harvest and transportation back home and when faced with war...he did what he was trained to do, scatter. We owe him our lives. He did use my connection to the Short-necks, not only to win this war but to communicate the terms of their surrender. I am yet to read all of the details but from what I hear they will never forget the victors of this war as they will carry our symbol wherever they go.

I would like to take this opportunity to thank you for looking after my Maggie. I have heard from Wilson that you have been with her almost every night. I rest easy knowing that you have been an honourable bird by keeping the males that were too lazy to fight in the war away from her. I thank you also for your patience and continual preservation of all my work. I will be returning before the year is done so I can spend some time with Maggie before heading back out west to resume my research. I would like you to ponder on the idea of coming with me, not as an assistant but as a full partner. Please consider my request.

I currently do not feel the urge to fill you in on absolutely everything. Not only because I have run out of resources once again but because these celebrations have become a distraction.

Until we meet again.

William J Whistlebeak

December 14th, 1932
From Celene Long-toe
to her husband Edward

Dearest Edward

The excitement cannot be contained here at home with everyone celebrating after hearing the wonderful news. Did they really agree to all the terms of surrender?

The children are ecstatic at the thought of seeing their Father for the very first time. I have held off naming them until you return. This way you will be sure to imprint on them. They will know their father.

Do not delay in returning, my husband. There is so much for us to talk about and to be honest..I sometimes worry about writing so many letters. You never know who might read them in the future. What if the Short-necks get hold of them? The very thought makes me uncomfortable.

I know how busy you have been and I am sure there is still much work to be done so I will keep this letter short. I am filled with joy at the thought of seeing you again and starting our new journey together as a family.

With all my love,

Celene Long-toe

Dearest husband

My wings are spread out and my feet kick up dust as I dance at the news of victory. I am somewhat concerned that you are yet to send me this news yourself. Edward, being so fond of you I thought would give your letter priority but not to worry. There must be so much happening out there to distract you or perhaps you are planning to deliver me the news yourself. Either way, I am filled with joy at the thought of seeing you. And the children, oh, the children are beyond excited. I caught Florence trying to fly by leaping off a tree branch. How she got up there in the first place I have no idea but the stories we have heard from the war have made the next generation believe they are invincible. I am not the only mother waiting for her husband to return and talk some sense into our children. It has been too long and I cannot wait for life to return to normalcy.

We have missed you greatly and I am sure you are tired of hearing it but I will never grow tired of saying it.

I pray All Feather returns you home safely soon.

Greta Feathers

December 15th, 1932
From Maggie R Whistlebeak
to her husband William

Dear William

Celebrations have been going on ever since the news of your victory reached us. With the burden of war now gone you will be able to focus more on your work. Do you plan on returning home anytime soon or stay and conduct more research? I have survived this long without you so what is a few months more? Whatever decision you make know that I fully support you and that the children and I are being well looked after.

The caterpillars have been in abundance of late. Henry even took the children out and taught them what to look for when searching for one hiding in fruit. A method he learnt from you if I am not mistaken. The children are becoming quite the gatherers.

I will not bore you with the details, William. I know how busy you are. We love and think of you often.

Maggie R Whistlebeak

Official Terms of surrender signed by
the Short-necks on December11th 1932

We the undersigned, belonging to the Army of the Short-necks, having this
day surrendered to the Mob lead by General Edward R Long-toe, do solemnly
swear to lay down our weapons and never raise them to a member of the Mob
again, with the strict exception of civilians defending themselves. As
requested, we will proudly wear the Mob's symbol upon our shoulders, along
with the symbol of the bouncers, in all future wars. The Mob will be given
full access to the Short-neck society and will be provided with whatever
resources they need to travel far and wide. Food will also be provided in
paper bags whenever possible and free of charge.

Finally, No war, directly or indirectly, may be declared on the Mob or any of
the All Feather's creatures ever again, with the exception of the banana loving
Tree Swingers that recently escaped from the Short-neck prison.

7

AFTER WAR

"As we return to something resembling normality may we never forget what lead us to war. Food."

Percival Headsand

FINAL EDITION

  # THE DAILY MOB

★★ EST 1901　　★★★★★★★★★　　★★ 16 DEC 1932

MOB TAKES STEPS TOWARDS FULL PEACE

SLY FLYER'S NEW PERSPECTIVE

Shirley O'genus has spent her nights like any other sly flyer eating fruit and soaring through the darkened sky. Now her curiosity has gotten the better of her and she has landed amongst the mob. "It is quite surprising to me that no one has noticed the similarities between us." She said "We both like fruit. That is pretty significant." Shirley wants to learn about all of the things we have in common. She can be found every evening meeting with various members of the mob. She is very approachable so don't be afraid to say hello if you see her.

Column by Norman McWhistle

It has not been long since the war with the Short-necks came to an end but that has not stopped those willing to move forward in the direction of full peace. Many of the mob have stuck around out west to help with repairing some of the extensive damage. The most common request from short-necks is help with repairing something they call a fence. An odd thing that appears to be designed to keep unwanted visitors from eating their food supplies. Some speculate on the effectiveness of such a thing as our cousins can simply fly over it as well as Bouncers being able to leap over it and Hoppers burrow under it. "These short-necks, or Roberts as they like to be called, have some strange methods." said William J whistlebeak who has recently begun an anthropological study on the Short-necks

"For example. They wish to keep us out of their crops but fail to realise how high we can jump. It would be simpler to just ask us to stay clear." William hopes to publish his first volume on the Short-necks in the coming months. As peace grows between our two nations so does the curiosity of those who wish to learn of each other's cultures and customs. The High Mob has been rumoured to be working on delegating mob members to live amongst the Shortnecks to give a more visible peace to both nations. A notion that seems to cause devision in the mob.

nations. A notion that seems to cause some devision amongst the Mob.

Column by Audrey E Quillington

THE JOKE OF THE DAY

Did you hear about the featherless one who got a job in a short-neck school?
He was the Hall Monitor

PERSONAL COLUMN

Anthony. Have you ever danced with a devil? Have you thought about the actions that led you to where you are? There is a lot we can say about the way you bob your head, the way you run & the way you leap. We can take you one step further. We can give you the ability to fly but you already know that. Reaching out to us was the best & worst decision of your life. You won't regret this, Anthony. Your best life starts now. We will talk

16 February, 1933
From the desk of President Edward R Long-toe
at Fort John Written by his own foot

Dearest Greta

They say as the leader of nations I should let others handle what they call the

small details. My adviser William assured me that is how things should be

done. And so I let my second in command, General Headsand, deliver to you

John's affects and the nations condolences. I now realise this was done out of

my own cowardice as I was contempt to stick my head in the sand. My

beloved wife often wrote to me telling me how you and John represented all

that is good in the Long-neck society and I should use my power to ensure

that the hardest fighting would not fall on John's wings. For the longest part

of the war this was the case, to my great shame it was not enough. It has been

many months since I have been elected by twenty one votes, twenty one...

this number does not make sense to me but William assures me it will change

how we count. There are twenty one stars in the sky, twenty one grains of

sand in the desert. Twenty one units of water in a lake. I will admit it does

make things easier. I initially thought this system was flawed as there was no

way in feathers you voted for my rise to power. Once I had been advised you

did, I wept, truly you are all my wife says you to be.

While this letter will not bring back John or put fruit on the table, I hope it

will still bring you some comfort in the words I say. It is my understanding

you have been petitioning the courts of the Mob to release details of the final

battle and how your husband died and that the courts have told you this is

classified and I quote 'only a letter from the president himself will make us

unseal them'. As I am in fact the president, I will have sent the request to unseal those records and have enclosed a copy in this correspondence to you. Do what you wish with the knowledge that John, even in death, is the greatest amongst us. I can only speak on the personal side of that battle. It was the quick thinking and leadership of John that the ambush on my headquarters failed. Our tiny nation owes its very birth to John. If I was the Bird that John was I would be handing this letter to you myself, however as it is so clearly evident, I fall short of John..

May the All Feather bless you and bless us with the bloodline of John and that of his kin.

Forever the humble servant,
President Edward R Long-toe

24th May, 1933
From the desk of William J Whistlebeak
to Edward R Long-toe

Dear Edward

As I look back on all we have accomplished, from the expedition out west to your presidency and the war we fought between. I am reminded of how even the most stubborn can remove their heads from the sand and become something new. Much like how the stripes of youth fade as we grow old making us wiser. Your influence has spread through our nation at the great displeasure of the High Mob. There is no one you have influenced more than myself. All I ever wanted to be was a free thinking bird. One looking from the outside in, only ever wanting to study all aspects of life and record it for whoever is intrigued enough to learn.

I now stand where I never thought I would. Not only seeking to learn more but to defend what I already know. You brought that out in me and I am ever so grateful for it.

So many look up to you, Edward. The chicks write plays about you and the papers sing your praises. Your accomplishments are historic and yet there is still so much more to be done. This is why, as your adviser and your friend, I beseech you, do not stand down as leader of the Free Mob. Surely you can see that no one else is fit to take your place. In fact, I am quite certain I would have to resign alongside you. Something I have no trouble doing as it would finally give me the time to finish my research on the Short-necks.

I have never been one for sentiment but this letter is scattered with it. It has taken every feather on my body to write these words. The Mob is not ready for you to resign, nor I. I am not sure how many more times I need to say it. Promise me you will think long and hard on the decision you are making. It will effect us all.

No matter the outcome, it has been an honour to serve alongside you, Edward. May the All Feather bless and keep you.

William J Whistlebeak

28th may, 1933
From the desk of president Edward R long-toe to
William J Whistlebeak.

To my dearest friend William

As I write this letter I find it odd that as I look up from my desk, there you are counting away, scribbling something down about the Short-necks and organising something grand. As I read your recommendation of the draft, conscripting one bird in ten to join the Mob forces. While I think the idea has merit it begs the question why did we fight so hard if it was not to lead every bird to decide their own fate? I know what we have won but I am not foolish to think we won't be fighting again. I will not stand the Mob down from its current size but nor will I commit to training more of our young. Let them enjoy their stripes a bit longer. This new nation of the Mobs is young but it has to be built on something stronger than one bird and that bird should not be me. We need to show them. We need to show them what I did. Rising through the ranks is something any bird can do. I think about the old High Mob. They were in power until their children lost their stripes and took over. This is not the kind of ideal that we fought and died for. When I step down, I do so to show them. To show them that power, that every corruptible fruit, that every seductive caterpillar can be turned down and the very same bird that took the highest office is the same bird that leaves with a smile on his beak. I am pleased that you will resign when I step down as a matter of fact I would ask you step down in twenty days time. Not to pick up your studies in the Short-necks, while I think you do great work there I believe I have a better idea of what you could do with your time. Run for office my good bird. Become the President of the nation that you and I built. I know many of the Mob think you are not best suited for the role and that your failings at home confirm this. I would tell them in the strongest words I have...I whole heartily disagree. You once asked me what the R stands for in my name and why on the official records my name is Edward R Long-toe. I did not tell you. I know you saw that as a sign that I did not trust you. Well I trust you and here it is. The R doesn't stand for anything. When I joined my first mob I was so nervous I wrote my name down wrong. It was the first time, in fact, I had ever written my name and I was too ashamed to correct it. As always, if you tell anyone this I will kick you in the chest. Good luck on your presidential campaign.

Edward R long-toe

MISSING MOB MYSTERY

The Infamous striper killer has been a mystery that began long before the war. Detective Lawrence Wynd has been working the case since its beginning and now believes the same killer is responsible for the six mob members that went missing early last week. "The similarities are uncanny." said Wynd in his latest press conference "If you changed the names on both cases you wouldn't be able to tell the difference." Wynd has been a very good boy with piecing it all together, despite the culprit continuing to evade capture. Wynd believes that if the striper killer has branched out to the mob then the chances of them being caught are much higher.

"When someone becomes overconfident, mistakes are made." said Wynd "I am not barking up the wrong tree on this one. This case will be closed before the year is out." While many have questions for Wynd he remains silent. Refusing to answer what he calls 'tail chasing questions.' One thing remains true. The Mystery of the missing mob will be solved and those responsible will be brought to justice in the name of the All Feather.

Column by Audrey E Quillington

SWOOPING SEASON BROUGHT FORWARD

Heather McDiver has recently taken leadership of the tidings and has brought in some controversial decisions. As we know, swooping season has always been in the later months and is done to protect their young, mostly from those who have the inability to climb trees but that is not enough according to McDiver. "Why should we only protect our young? Surely our homes are worthy of protecting too." She said in a heated interview. "If it were up to me we would be swooping all year long. I have made compromises and so should everyone else." Complaints have come from all over the place with reports of even Tunnellers being swooped

. Some are worried that a war may start between the mob and the tidings, something worth avoiding due to our cousin's air superiority. While an official meeting will be organised by our nations we can only hope that McDiver will be open to compromise.

Column by Norman McWhistle

PERSONAL COLUMN

Mother, there is no easy way to say this. The war changed me.

. I was sent against my will but ended up embracing it. I had a moments peace when I returned but with the mob under attack by a hidden enemy I must take things into my own wings. P

8

FATE OF THE FEATHERED

(AND FRIENDS)

Edward R Long-toe rose through the ranks at a very fast rate and became President of the Mob while still maintaining his position as commander of the Alliance between Bouncers and Long-necks. He stood down as President in 1933 to allow others the opportunity to lead the nation of mobs. He died peacefully in his sleep at age 13. He is remembered and revered as the greatest leader in mob history.

Percival Headsand embraced the soldier inside. Upon returning home he could not sit still for very long and as soon as he heard reports of his fellow mob members going missing he set out to discover who was behind it. He was last seen delivering a personal column entry to the Daily Mob on January 2nd 1933.

John Feathers was killed in the line of duty. He saved many of his fellow mob and is arguably the sole reason for the Short-neck's surrender. He is survived by his wife Greta, son Philip, son Richard, son Thomas, daughter Joan, daughter Helen, son Walter, daughter Alice, son Jerry, son Earl, daughter Jane, son Wayne, daughter Florence and son Howard.

William J Whistlebeak returned home to discover his assistant Henry in a compromising position with his wife Maggie. He left without a word and headed back out west to finish his work with the Short-necks. He lived among them for a time but as adviser to the president he was called home often. When Edward stood down as president he was encouraged to run for office. William served two terms and was well received by the nation. He died peacefully in his sleep age 9. Sadly he never finished his 7th volume of his anthropologic study on Short-necks. However, his great great great great great granddaughter Delilah expressed some interest in finishing his work.

Greta Feathers never remarried. She raised 13 children on her own and did not stop there. She took many strays under her wings and was known as Mother to all. Much like John, she was well admired by the Mob at large. She died peacefully in her sleep aged 11. She is survived by her 163 grandchildren and her 1948 great grandchildren.

Maggie R Whistlebeak stayed with Henry for the summer but then separated when she discovered him in a compromising position with her sister. She then attempted to reconnect with William but was unsuccessful due to his heavy work schedule. She married George Lyre in 1934. The marriage lasted 8 months due to George finding her in a compromising position with George's son, Peter. She then married Peter in 1935. They stayed together until Maggie's passing in 1939. She died in her sleep aged 10.

Celene Long-toe stood by her husband Edward through thick and thin. She was known as the bird behind the bird. It was rumoured that she wrote all his speeches but it can be neither confirmed nor denied. She outlived her husband 4 years and continued to tell of his accomplishments until her passing.

Detective Lawrence Wynd never solved the mystery of the Striper Killer or the missing mob members. He was close to solving it though and kept reminding folks of the fact right up until his death in 1936. His last solved mystery was finding out who the good boy was. Him.

EMU TERMINOLOGY

- Short-Neck - Human
- Long-neck - Emu
- All Feather - The Emu God
- First Wing - First hand
- Cousin - Any bird other than an Emu.
- Hopper - Rabbit
- Bouncer - Kangaroo
- Featherless ones - Goannas
- Prickly Ant eater - Echidna
- Invisible Ants - Termites
- Tree Hugger - Koala
- Striper - Tasmanian Tiger
- Mini Striper - Numbat
- Howler - Dingo
- Tunnellers (or Digger) - Wombat
- Glider - Sugar Glider
- Sly Flyer - Fruit Bat
- Screamer - Fox
- Screecher - Cockatoo
- LCM's (Laughing Cousin Mimics) - Machine Guns
- Tree Swinger - Gorilla

Made in the USA
Middletown, DE
02 June 2022